Lucky Duck

Barbara deRubertis
Illustrated by Eva Vagreti Cockrille

The Kane Press
New York

Cover Design: Sheryl Kagen

Library of Congress Catalog Card Number: 96-75015

ISBN 1-57565-004-5

10 9 8 7 6 5

First published in the United States of America in 1997 by The Kane Press.
Printed in China.

LET'S READ TOGETHER is a registered trademark of The Kane Press.

Lucky Duck
can jump and run.
Lucky Duck
is having fun.

Buzzy Bug says,
"Look out, Lucky!
Don't run where
the mud is mucky!"

Lucky runs.

Lucky stumbles.

6

Lucky bumps.

Lucky tumbles.

Lucky gets a
muddy dunk.
Now poor Lucky
Duck is sunk!

Buzzy Bug says,
"Lucky Duck!
You have just run
out of luck!

"You are not a
LUCKY duck!
You are just a
MUCKY duck!

"Get up! Get up!"
says Buzzy Bug.
Lucky gives a
muddy shrug.

"Buzzy, I am just a dud. I am *stuck* here in this mud!"

Buzzy says, "When
you are stuck,
you can't just trust
in luck, old Duck!

"Don't give up
and do not fuss.
I will bring
your buddy Gus."

Gus the Gull
and Buzzy Bug
give Lucky Duck
a mighty tug.

But Lucky Duck
still is stuck
in the grubby
mud and muck.

"Look up! Look up!"
says Buzzy Bug.
"Your puppy chums
have come to tug.

"Rusty Pup and
Dusty Pup
have come to help us
tug you up!"

The chums all tug.
They huff and puff.
They huff and puff
and puff and huff.

Lucky makes a
thumpy thud.
He blubs and glubs
in muddy mud.

UN-Lucky Duck
STILL is stuck.
This grubby duck
is out of luck!

And look who's come!
It's Stinky Skunk!
He drums his drum,
"Plunky plunk."

Stinky says,
"I'll have some fun!
I'll puff my stuff and
make them run!"

Rusty, Dusty,
Buzzy, and Gus
jump up and run.
"Don't puff on us!"

Lucky Duck
begins to cluck.
"I MUST not be a
stinky duck!"

As Stinky comes,
he hums and drums.
"Tum de dum de
PUM PUM PUM!"

Lucky *TUGS*....

Now he's UN-stuck!

Up he goes!
That **LUCKY DUCK!!**